New Born

Kathy Henderson
Illustrated by Caroline Binch

FRANCES LINCOLN

Look little baby,
I'll show you some shadows,
patches and patterns
of daylight and darkness
scattered all dapply on to the wall.

And that is your shawl
that's tickling and teasing
your sleepy soft cheek,

and there –
those strange things
that wave round in the air
are your fingers,
and that stuff they're tangling is hair.

Here, little baby,
the light swings and turns
as you ride through the house.
There are colours
and noises,
the tumble of voices,
a creak and a bang
as a bedroom door slams.

There is rustling, crackling,
paper unwrapping,
the click of a switch
and a whistling, flickering
picture that speaks.

And then there's the wind
that rattles and moans
and the startle-stop, startle-stop call
of the telephone.

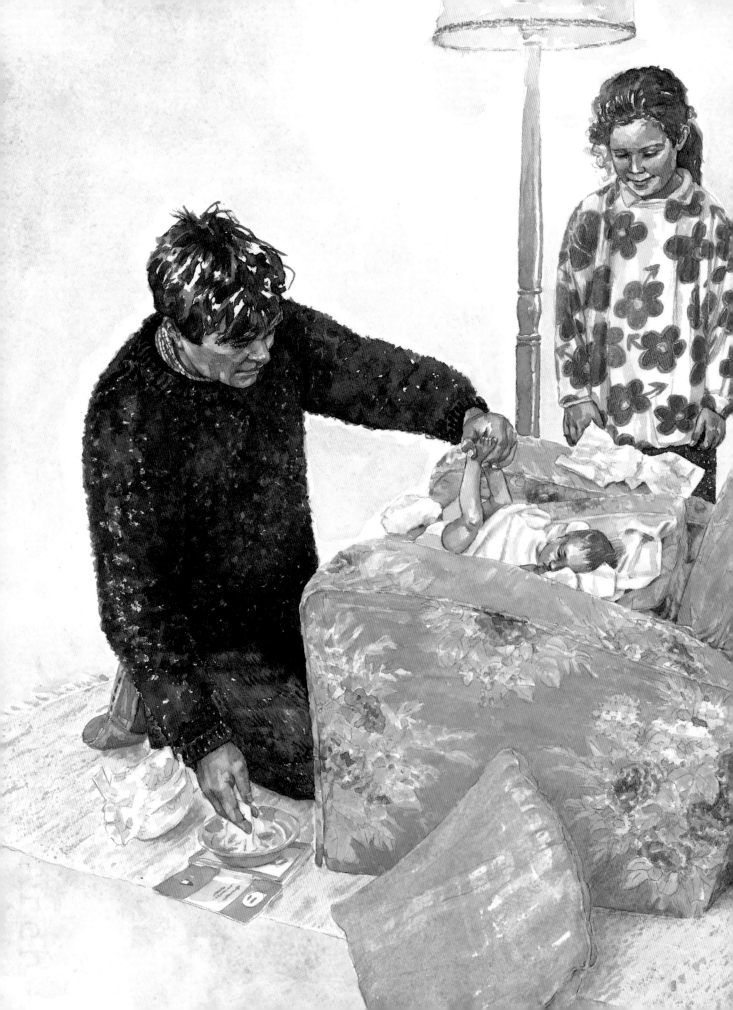

Come little baby, we'll sit down here.
This is a table
and this is a chair
and that's a light bulb glowing there,

and that coloured shape
is the wing of a flower,
and that snaky line
is a strand of white string,

and there's the ring of the bell at the door,
and here's Aunt Ella, bringing you more,
even more flowers.

And this is the fur
and the tail and the whiskers,
this is the purr of the fireside cat.

And now you hear laughter –
your brother is teasing,
and a-a-a-WHOO-SHOO!
your father is sneezing.

And those sounds are music –
look, you can dance too,
and there, that's a mirror,
and that baby's you.

Here little baby, look up high.
This is a window,
and out there's the sky
and the sun and the wind
and the rain and the clouds
and cars and people and houses and lights,
and at night there are stars.
Out there's the whole world.

And this?
It's the edge of the curtain flapping,
blue cloth with patterns.

And this is a hug, and this is a kiss,
and this is the end of it all for now,
because here's your cradle
and here's your warm shawl.

Sleep, little baby,
who knows what you've seen
or what worlds you dream of,
so small and new born.

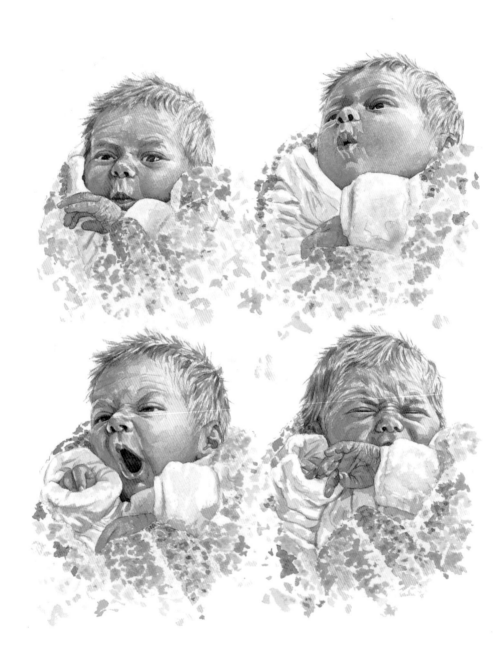

For Gabriel Finn
and the Dolphins, Kia and Teagan • *CB*

British Library Cataloguing in Publication Data
available on request

ISBN 0-7112-1262-7

Set in Garamond 3
Printed in Hong Kong
9 8 7 6 5 4 3 2 1